D0884115

LITTLE PIERROT

3 STARRY EYES

Library of Congress Control Number: 2018933607
ISBN: 978-1-941302-62-0

Super-slowness is such a sad superpower!

What about me, then?
Am I invisible? Do I have a superpower, too?

That's exactly how I feel!

Hey, Mister Snail!

I said... Hey, Mister Snail!

Why aren't you saying anything? Are you mad at me?
And I'm the crazy one?

Well, let me know when you're done sulking...
But... I'm talking to you!
Did you become deaf? ...In love?

My lemon tree is the most handsome...

No, my orange tree is! It's perfect!

Nuh uh!
My prune tree is the prettiest...

Little Pierrot?
Uh...
I see three trees...
All from the same garden.

Emily, did you know that poppies dream while they sleep? I read it in a book.

And did you know that water lilies exist in all the colors of the universe?

Isn't it beautiful?
It's very beautiful, Little Pierrot. Very beautiful, but...

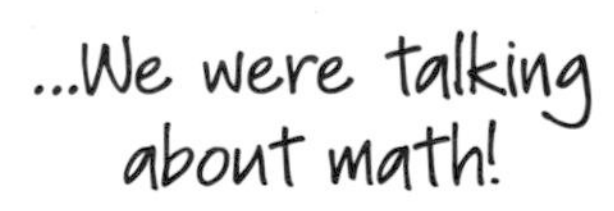
...We were talking about math!

I'm very impressed!

By the light of the moOOOOOOOOON

AAATCHAAA

What are you doing?
We're trying to break the record for biggest booger...

Do you want to try?

WHOA!
That's so disgusting.

Good job, Little Pierrot. You win...

Psh! Beginner's luck...

I'm dreaming
I'm dreaming
I'm dreaming!

And it's not over yet!

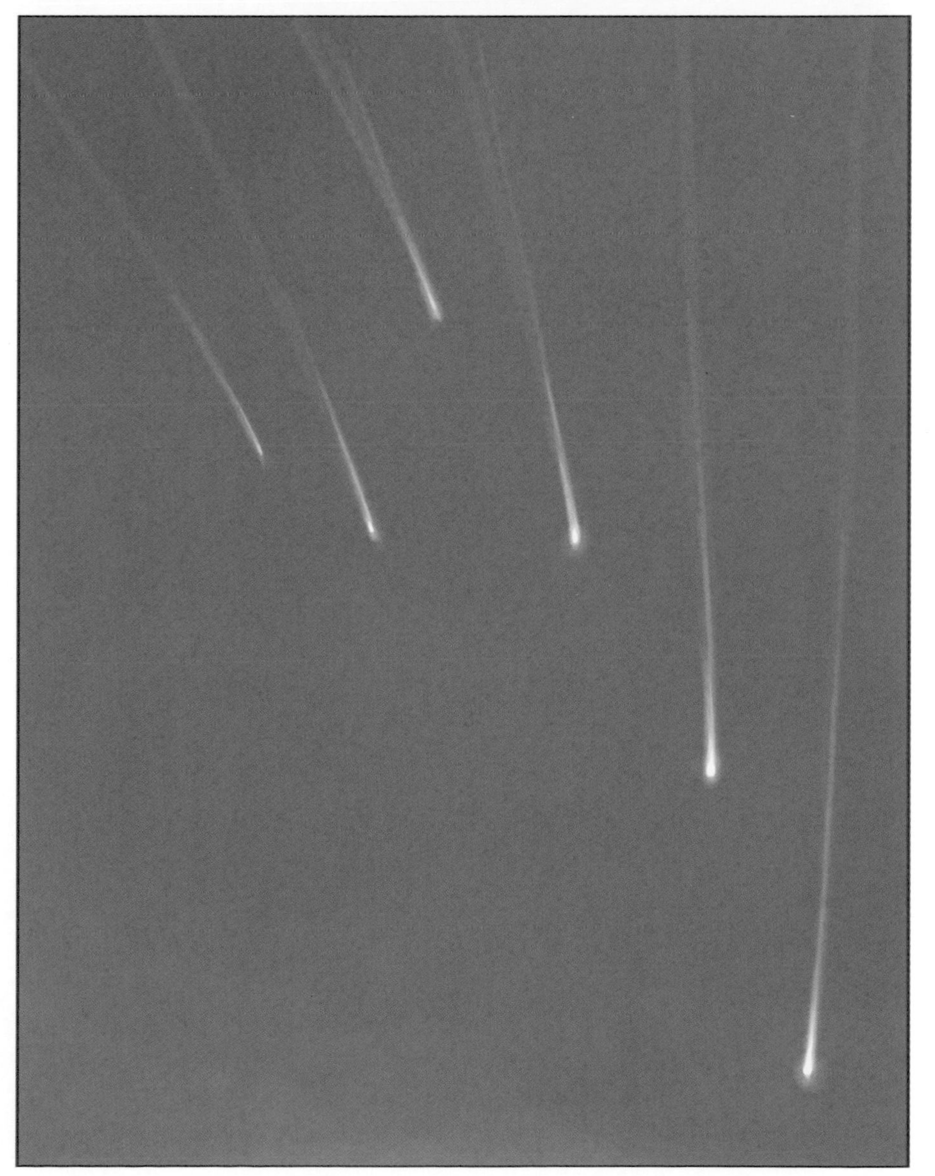

What is that?
A bomb!
It's ugly!
Some people say we'd just have to give it a reason to make it more...
...Human?

V like Verbose

Adj. (latin: verbosum,
from verbum meaning "word")
Using or containing more words than
necessary to express an idea

You have to be aware of the magnitude of the work ahead of you. Making a dictionary is a Herculean task. You'll have to be clear and precise. You have to respect the French and the Latin, and not lose sight that food for thought must be delicious and never inedible and...

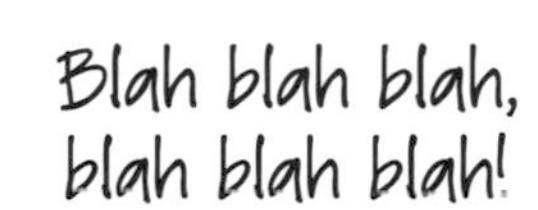

Three more questions.

What is the largest bird in the world?

...

The great albatross?

Very good, Emily!

And who can name the largest aquatic mammal?

A blue whale, teacher...

And, lastly, does anyone know the name of the Earth's natural satellite?

Me! Me!
I know! Me! Me!
I
Me!

Hey, Mister Snail!
Hey, Emily!

You can see him?
Of course.
And you can hear him, too?
Obviously...

And can you see that?
Yeah, but that's only normal. It's huge.

What about you, Little Pierrot, can you see that?

Ha ha ha!
Yes! Yes!

And... can you hear that?
Yes!
BOBOM
BOBOM
BOBOM

It's Fall, my favorite season!
Because we can play hide-and-seek under the leaves?
Ha ha ha... No, Mister Snail! Because you can still see Miss Moon even from behind the trees!

D like Doubtful

Adj. (latin: dubitare, from dubito meaning "doubt")
Giving rise to doubt or uncertainty; skeptical, incredulous

Hey, Mister Snail... Tonight, I'm making dinner!

Are we celebrating something?

A like Amicable

Adj. Characterized by or showing goodwill, being agreeable. An amicable man – Amicable words.

I wonder what could be behind it?

This door is always closed...

...Maybe there's something amazing, incredible, extraordinary.
Maybe I should try to open it?

It's up to you... But you can't forget that a closed door is a door open to your imagination.
You're right, Mister Snail...

...After all, there were probably just adults behind the door!

What is that?
It's a cemetery...
What's a cemetery?
When people die, they're buried here...

You mean we put them underground?
Well... yes!

Why do we put them underground if afterward they go up to the sky?

Some things are inexplicable, but we still explain them to kids...

Mister Snail, I've got an impossible riddle for you...
Can you tell me what's in my box?
For me?

A sheep?
How...? Mister Snail, you cheated! You read my book!

I want a dog!
I'm right here!
But I'd like a "best friend"...

And it would be annoying to walk you on a leash...

Meet Norbert, my chihuahua.
Oooh! He's so cute! He's shaking so much...

KAÏ
KAÏ
KAÏ

WAF
WAFF
RRRR
WAF
WAF
No, Norbert! Be nice!

Your snail should be on a leash!
Ah, "man's best friend" is just great! How brave and elegant...

Watch closely, Little Pierrot!

If I do...

THIS!
PLOP!

It's too funny...

Why doesn't he look happy?
Why isn't he saying anything?

It wasn't my fault!
You didn't say anything, either...
You didn't say any-thing to stop him!

M like MOON

n. (luna) 1 - Natural satellite of the Earth. New moon: phase of the moon when, while in between the sun and the Earth, it looks invisible.

2 - Moonstruck: being distracted - Asking, promising the moon: asking, promising the impossible - Over the moon: being extremely happy about an unexpected event - Honeymoon: A happy time couples spend together after marriage.

L like Love
v. (amor) 1 - Feeling a profound affection for someone, a deep attachment. 2 - Feeling a deep inclination toward someone based on tenderness and physical attraction. 3 - Having a penchant, or taste, for something. 4 - To better like: prefer. 5 - To feel or show mutual affection.

Say, Little Pierrot...
What is Miss Moon
hanging from?
I can't tell you...
So I'll whisper it
to you instead.